DISCARD

DISCARD

D1297059

To God be the glory!

For Nino, Nick, and Nate.
Love you. Always.
—Kris


For Freya and Sonia.
—Cori

# BE MY ValenSLIME

written by
**KRIS TARANTINO**

illustrated by
**CORI DOERRFELD**

WATERBROOK

MEET THE MONSTERS!

R0467423328

A tad **gruffy**. A bit **grumpy**.

And definitely not **lovey-dovey**.

Which makes Snoodle an unusual monster.

But monsters **DON'T DO** Valentine's Day!

"We're **tough!**" says Iggy.

"Love's **icky!**" snaps Zee-Zee.

BOMP!

CLOMP!

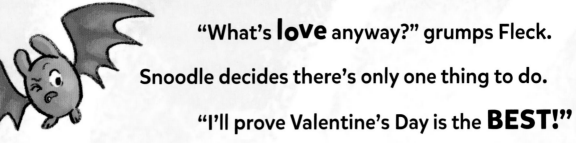

"What's **love** anyway?" grumps Fleck.

Snoodle decides there's only one thing to do.

"I'll prove Valentine's Day is the **BEST!**"

STOMP!

When Snoodle tries to show her
friends how to decorate a box . . .

The monsters go WILD!

But Snoodle keeps her cool in the chaos.
After all, love is patient.

**OOPS.** Monsters aren't good with scissors . . . but without an opening, where will the valentines go?

Fleck knows just what to do:
use his claws to cut!

It's not exactly what Snoodle pictured . . . but that's okay.
Because love is always kind—and never rude.

Nothing is better than balloons! Monsters **love** balloons.

**OH NO!** Not many balloons are left.

Snoodle is upset, but then she counts to ten.

"Forget balloons," she tells Zee-Zee. "Let's try blowing bubblegum bubbles instead."

Because love isn't quick to get angry.

Maybe decorating with streamers will be easier!

**Wowza!** That's a lot of tangled-up, taped-up monsters! This isn't working out the way Snoodle hoped.

She can't help but giggle, though.

Because even when things get
sticky, love doesn't remember mistakes.

It's cupcake and cookie time!

Everyone gets in the **groove!**

# OH MY! More monster messes.

But Snoodle knows a few globs of frosting don't matter.
Because love looks at more than just the outside.

It sees the **heart**.

Looking around, Snoodle realizes this party is nothing like she imagined. It's too **messy**, too **sticky**, too **monster-y** to be perfect.

But then Snoodle remembers . . .

love doesn't have to be perfect.

One more thing will make this party just right. Snoodle rolls out some fancy paper and searches for the perfect words.

Burp with Me, Valentine!

Me Eat You Up!

Bug Breath!

Cute & Creepy!

Monsterific!

Because love always trusts . . .

always hopes . . . always keeps trying . . .

until it feels **just right.**

And before you know it . . . love changes you.

Because love always finds a way.

# EVEN FOR MONSTERS.